Library of Congress Control Number: 2021901615

ISBN: 978-1-68369-286-7

Printed in China

Typeset in Miller and Gill Sans
Designed by Elissa Flanigan
Story adapted by Rebecca Gyllenhaal, based on the series created by Arlene Klasky, Gábor Csupó, and Paul Germain and the episode "A Rugrats Chanukah" written by J. David Stem and David N. Weiss
Production management by John J. McGurk

Quirk Books
215 Church Street
Philadelphia, PA 19106

quirkbooks.com

10 9 8 7 6 5 4 3 2 1

A Rugrats chanukah

Based on the series created by Arlene Klasky, Gábor Csupó, and Paul Germain and the episode "A Rugrats Chanukah" written by J. David Stem and David N. Weiss

Illustrated by Kim Smith

QUIRK BOOKS

PHILADELPHIA

Tommy, Chuckie, Phil, Lil, and Angelica
were playing in Tommy's living room.
But it wasn't an ordinary playdate.
Something about today was different.

Tommy's mom was making pancakes for dinner, and his Grandma Minka
was reading them a story about the Jewish people.

Long ago, in the land of Israel, the Jewish people lived happily
with their neighbors, the ancient Greeks. But one day a new king
of the Greeks arrived and wanted everyone to be just like him.
He told the Jewish people they had to wear the same clothes,
read the same books, and worship the same gods as him.

A hero stepped forward to challenge the king. His name was Judah, and he was the leader of the Maccabees, a group of brave Jewish warriors.

He was a brave leader, and he led his people against
the powerful armies of the evil king.

Just as the story was getting exciting, Grandma Minka closed the book and went into the kitchen to help Tommy's mom fry the latkes for the Chanukah fair.

"Potatoes, water, and salt? These just don't seem like pancakes,"
Chuckie's dad said.

"They're potato pancakes," Tommy's mom said. "We fry these, and sometimes
doughnuts, to remind us of the oil used in the miracle of Chanukah."

"Something funny is going on," Tommy said. "Mom's making pancakes at nighttime. My grandma read us that story about the Maccababies. And my grandpa gave us chocolate money and these cradles!"

"And that's not all," he said. "Every night I have to wear a funny hat while Grandpa Boris says some stuff I don't understand and Mom lights another candle. And then I get a present!"

"Dumb babies!" Angelica said. "Those candles aren't for Tommy's birthday. Those are for Chanukah!"

"Harmonica?" Tommy asked.

"Chanukah is that special time of year between Christmas and Misgiving, when all the bestest holiday shows are on TV," Angelica explained. "Now get out of the way! It's time for my TV special!"

"Kids, it's time to go to synagogue!" said
Tommy's mom. "Grandpa Boris is going to be in
a play all about the meaning of Chanukah."

"Phooey!" Grandpa Boris said.
"This play will be the end of me!"

The babies crowded around the newspaper that Grandpa Boris dropped. The man in the photo looked scary. "The meany of Chanukah!" the babies said.

"I had to play with a meany at daycare once," Chuckie said. "He put a worm on my head!"

"That's it, then!" said Tommy. "Grandpa Boris needs our help. We've got to put the meany of Chanukah down for a nap!"

Before the play, the family went to the Chanukah fair.
The babies looked all around, but they didn't see the
meany of Chanukah anywhere.

Angelica tried a latke but quickly spat it out. "Yuck! Topatoes!" she said. "What kind of bobo-head makes pancakes out of topatoes?"

"I don't get it! We've looked everywhere!" Tommy said.

"It's hard to find the meany of Chanukah," Phil said.

Then the curtain rose and the play began. A man stomped on stage and pointed his sword at Grandpa Boris. The babies gasped. It was the meany of Chanukah!

The babies bravely rushed onstage
to save Grandpa Boris!

But the grown-ups quickly caught them, and the babies
were sent to the nursery for the rest of the play.

"We were trying to save Grandpa Boris from the meany of Chanukah,
but the grown-ups wouldn't let us!" Tommy explained.

Angelica didn't care about the meany of Chanukah. She just wanted to
escape so she could watch her favorite Christmas special on TV.

"I have an idea," Angelica said. "You don't need blankies and stuff to put a grown-up down for a nap. You know what you need?"

Angelica freed the babies from the nursery and led them into the janitor's office, where she had seen a TV before she was locked in the nursery. "The onlyest thing a grown-up needs is a TV," she whispered.

Together, the babies boosted Angelica to the top of the shelf.

"Careful, that's my soft spot!" said Lil.

"Your whole head is a soft spot," Angelica grumbled.

Angelica grabbed the TV, but tumbled
all the way down to the floor!

"Come on you guys, Grandpa needs us!"
Tommy said.

"Not so fast, babies!" Angelica said.
"This TV is mine!"

"But Angelica, what about the meany of Chanukah?" Tommy shouted.

"Stupid babies," Angelica shouted back. "There *is* no meany of Chanukah!"

Just then, Angelica ran smack into a
grown-up and fell flat on her butt!

Angelica burst into tears.

"What's happening?" Chuckie asked.

"I think the meany's trying to squeeze her guts out!" Phil said.

"What do we do?!" Lil said.

Phil used Tommy's pillowcase to pretend he was a ghost to scare the meany away, but that plan didn't work so well. "That wasn't very scary," Lil said.

Tommy had an idea. He remembered how Grandpa Boris fell asleep every time he read a good story. He held up his *My First Chanukah* book, hoping that if the meany of Chanukah read it, he would take a nap.

Just then, Grandpa Boris found them.

"The kinderlach want you to finish the story!" he said to the meany.

So, the meany of Chanukah sat down and began to read.

And so, against all odds, Judah the Maccabee won the right for his people to live and learn in the way of their ancestors. But after the war, the people of Israel had a difficult job. Though the king of the Greeks had been driven from their land, he had left their cities and their holy Temple in a terrible mess.

The meany of Chanukah paused the story.

"A menorah is like the night-light of our people," he said. "In times of darkness, it shines on the whole world, reminding us not to be afraid to be different, but to be proud of who we are. It was filled with oil, which makes it burn, but today some people use candles instead."

The Jewish people repaired their Temple, but the Greeks had left only enough oil to burn in the menorah for one night. They lit the menorah anyway. What the people needed was a miracle.

Yeah, a miracle. Whatever that is.

But one day went by, and then
another, and another.

Until, finally, eight days had passed. The flames were still burning.

The story had put the meany of Chanukah to sleep, just as Tommy said it would. Grandpa Boris read the end of the story.

"And to this day, we light the menorah every year to remember the miracle of Chanukah."

Just then, the curtain rose and the babies saw that they were on stage.
The grown-ups sat in the audience, looking very surprised to see them.

When the meany of Chanukah woke up and saw the audience, he quickly stood and said, "And so ends our little play! May it be our sincerest Chanukah wish that our little kinderlach will continue to carry the light of our people for generations to come."

"Look, Tommy, the meany of Chanukah and your Grandpa
Boris are playing nice!" Chuckie said.

"I know, Chuckie. It's a miracle!" Tommy said.

"Maybe they're having all your birthdays at the same time," said Phil.

"Maybe you're all growed up now and you gotta get a job," said Lil.
"Make a wish and blow the candles out!"

The babies lifted Tommy up to the very top of the TV. He was just about to blow out the candles when his cousin Angelica walked in.